Dear Parents:

Congratulations! Your child is taking the first steps on an exciting journey. The destination? Independent reading!

STEP INTO READING® will help your child get there. The program offers five steps to reading success. Each step includes fun stories and colorful art or photographs. In addition to original fiction and books with favorite characters, there are Step into Reading Non-Fiction Readers, Phonics Readers and Boxed Sets, Sticker Readers, and Comic Readers—a complete literacy program with something to interest every child.

Learning to Read, Step by Step!

Ready to Read   Preschool–Kindergarten
• big type and easy words • rhyme and rhythm • picture clues
For children who know the alphabet and are eager to begin reading.

Reading with Help   Preschool–Grade 1
• basic vocabulary • short sentences • simple stories
For children who recognize familiar words and sound out new words with help.

Reading on Your Own   Grades 1–3
• engaging characters • easy-to-follow plots • popular topics
For children who are ready to read on their own.

Reading Paragraphs   Grades 2–3
• challenging vocabulary • short paragraphs • exciting stories
For newly independent readers who read simple sentences with confidence.

Ready for Chapters   Grades 2–4
• chapters • longer paragraphs • full-color art
For children who want to take the plunge into chapter books but still like colorful pictures.

STEP INTO READING® is designed to give every child a successful reading experience. The grade levels are only guides; children will progress through the steps at their own speed, developing confidence in their reading. The F&P Text Level on the back cover serves as another tool to help you choose the right book for your child.

Remember, a lifetime love of reading starts with a single step!

To Lev
—J.R.

Text copyright © 2022 by Jean Reagan
Cover art and interior illustrations copyright © 2022 by Lee Wildish

Step into Reading, Random House, and the Random House colophon are registered trademarks of Penguin Random House LLC.

Visit us on the Web!
StepIntoReading.com
rhcbooks.com

Educators and librarians, for a variety of teaching tools, visit us at RHTeachersLibrarians.com

Library of Congress Cataloging-in-Publication Data is available upon request.
ISBN 978-0-593-47911-7 (trade) — ISBN 978-0-593-47912-4 (lib. bdg.) — ISBN 978-0-593-47913-1 (ebook)

Printed in the United States of America
10 9 8 7 6 5 4 3 2 1
First Edition

This book has been officially leveled by using the F&P Text Level Gradient™ Leveling System.

How to FIND THE TOOTH FAIRY

by Jean Reagan

illustrated by Lee Wildish

Random House 🏠 New York

I have a loose tooth.

Wiggle. Wiggle. Wiggle.

Look, Grandpa!
It came out!

Yay!
The Tooth Fairy
will give me money
for my tooth.

Oh, no!
The Tooth Fairy
will not find me.
I am not at my house.

11

I have an idea, Grandpa.

Let's make a sign.

Let's hang it
on the window.

Oh, no!
How will she
get in the window?

I have another idea!
We can leave it open
a crack.

Now she can get in.

I put my tooth
under the pillow,
Grandpa.

Now we are ready!

Do we see her flying?

Not yet.

She can only come

when we are sleeping.

Okay. Good night!

I hope
she will find me.

Good morning!
Look, Grandpa!

The Tooth Fairy came and left me some money!